Frederick's Fables

 *A Leo Lionni Treasury of Favorite Stories*

Frederick's Fables

with an introduction by Bruno Bettelheim

Pantheon Books

For Pippo, Annie, Sylvan, and Gina

Library of Congress Cataloging in Publication Data
Lionni, Leo. Frederick's fables.
Reprint of works originally published 1960–1983. Summary: A collection
of thirteen of Lionni's previously published books, presented in the
same format.   1. Children's stories, American.   [1. Animals—Fiction.
2. Short stories] I. Title. PZ7.L6634Fr 1985 [E] 85-5186
ISBN 0-394-87710-1   ISBN 0-394-97710-6 (lib. bdg.)
ISBN 0-394-87812-4 (ltd. ed.)

Contents

Introduction

Why do young children like picture books so much? What is their value for children, and their fascination?

Objective reality holds little attraction for the young child, because he cannot yet comprehend it adequately and fully, certainly not to his satisfaction. As patiently as a parent may try to explain matters to a child, the child can at best understand only fragments of the explanation he is given. Therefore, he tries to make sense of such fragments, elaborating them with figments of his imagination; he weaves fantasies around what he encounters in reality. When that which he derives from his imagination is applied to reality, reality begins to make more sense to him in ways that are in line with the development of his mind.

To accomplish this process, the child has recourse to his own experiences. Inert objects are invested with feelings and intentions similar to those the child knows best—his own. Since the child knows that when he moves about he does so for certain purposes, he imagines that whatever moves, such as a ball, also moves about for a purpose: to annoy the child, to look for a better place to rest, or to get something it desires. As the child wonders about the change from day to night and from one season to the next, or about who makes it rain, he is convinced that his dog or cat also wonders about such matters. The child assumes that his animals—real and stuffed—think and feel, hate and love, just as he does. He believes that they worry as he does, have hopes and fears similar to his, and experience disappointment as keenly as he does. And since seeing is believing, the pictures in a child's picture book that depict animals as having intentions and feelings like those of the child give credence to the child's view of the world.

The impressions of the world that the child thus receives are largely the product of his imagination, but it is an imagination that originates in what the child hears, what he feels, and, most important, what he sees. The ideas he develops on his own about what he sees—being based on his very limited experiences—are not only largely solipsistic but tend to be repetitive and quite meager in scope. It cannot be otherwise, given the narrowness of the child's experience of the world. Fortunately, the picture book is by no means so limited.

While the picture book reflects images of the world similar to those the child creates in his mind, these are not limited as is the child's own experience. In picture books the child encounters and becomes familiar with fantasies that others have woven around what is visible in the world. These fantasies are in some measure already familiar to the child, since he has had similar visual experiences of reality.

When these pictures in the book are not just illustrations that merely reflect what is told in the text accompanying them but are the creations of a real artist, these pictures are images which in one visual experience convey more than can be said in a thousand words. That is true for the pictures in Leo Lionni's books.

Such pictures are the result of a much richer, much more mature, and, most important, much more artistic imagination than the young child could muster on his own, given the limitations of his mind and experience. While these pictures deal with reality in a most imaginative way—as does the child—they do so with quite startlingly different results. Thus the child learns from them, to the great enrichment of his mind and his artistic sensibilities, that new fantasies can be spun around these familiar figures and objects. How exciting to the child's fantasies, and to his mind in general!

The best picture books exist first in the mind of the artist. These books contain relatively little text because whatever of significance they have to tell is conveyed through pictorial images. The words should say just enough to suggest the subject of the artist's fantasies, so that the child can share in the artist's imaginative visual fantasies, which have quite a different effect than fantasies which are conveyed mainly by words. If the text is too long or too complex, and the pictures are reduced to mere illustrations, then the fantasy is one best expressed through words and not through pictures. Word fantasies come from the imagination of an author—in the best of circumstances, a poet; but in that case the imagination is mainly a literary one rather than a painterly, visual one that can speak directly to the young child. When the child reaches a stage of development where he can comprehend and respond to and enjoy literary fantasies, then he has largely outgrown the age of the picture book. But to do so, he needs first to develop a rich and varied fantasy in images, since this is the precursor of a rich literary fantasy.

That such fantasy in images and pictures is our earliest and in many ways deepest fantasy, from which all later imagination develops, can be seen from the fact that we dream mostly in images. Only the wish to communicate these dream images to ourselves or others could force us to try to put them into words. If we should try to do so, we find that words, even those most carefully chosen, can convey at best only a little of the incredible richness contained in what we envision in our dreams. Only the artist who can think primarily in images can create true picture books.

Leo Lionni understands the importance of these visual images. He wrote in an article: "It is in the picture book that the child will have his first encounter with a structured fantasy," which he will "animate by his own feelings and imagery." Through the text of the story, as it is read aloud, Lionni says that the child "will discover the relationship between visual images and verbal language." The shorter the text, and the less it distracts from what can be seen in the image, the less it will interfere with the child's ability to "read" the pictures to his heart's content. Thus, in a true picture book, as in dreams and in the child's imagination, the visual image is primary, the text secondary. The pictures in *Frederick's Fables* are the creations of a truly adult mind which has retained—or regained—the ability to give body to imaginative visualizations, for which the artist draws heavily on his own childhood experiences. Leo Lionni's pictures add up to stories with meaning;

they tell the child things which are of significance to him. Thus they not only stimulate the child's imagination but suggest a deeper meaning. This enriches the child's imaginative existence and gives deeper meaning to the child's life.

It is the true genius of the artist that permits him to create picture images that convey meaning much deeper than that of the objects depicted. In Lionni's story "Fish Is Fish," the sequence of the pictures tells the child that two individuals who in their infancy are identical can, as they develop, become very different and distinct beings. This message can also be easily conveyed through words, but words could never convey as impressively another message inherent in these pictures, something of much greater importance for the young child's understanding of the world. This is the showing, through example, of how far our imagination can lead us astray when it is not corrected through direct experiences. In this story the frog tries to tell the fish about the world, which the fish has never seen. The information the frog gives about the beings who live in this world is all correct; still, what the fish imagines on the basis of what is told to him is shown to be way off the mark. The fish imagines that birds are fish with wings; cows are fish with four legs, two horns, and an udder; and that people are fish wearing clothes and walking upright on two legs. The pictures convey to the young child much more convincingly and dramatically than words possibly could how descriptions in words can totally mislead us.

The pictures in this story convey in the simplest and most direct form the insight of the ancient Greek philosopher who realized that if cows imagined gods, they would imagine them cowlike. Without necessarily recognizing it explicitly, the child learns implicitly from these pictures that as the fish imagines all other creatures in fishlike form, so the child in all probability makes the same error and imagines the rest of the world in terms of his own experience; and that it requires direct contact with reality, and its acceptance as valid, for us to escape seeing all things in a solipsistic manner. Compared with this important insight, which only the pictures can provide in full force, the obvious message—that a fish is best off in its own element, water—seems trite. This is how it ought to be with a true picture book: the pictures have to transmit the deepest meaning of the story.

Lionni's story about Frederick impresses one as a version of Aesop's famous fable of the Ant and the Grasshopper; but at the same time it is like an answer to that fable. And how commonplace is this ancient fable, which relies on words, when compared to the story of Frederick the mouse, which is told in pictures! Aesop's fable stresses the value of hard work and the dire consequences for those who shun it. But the fable of Frederick, who is the dreamer among the little field mice, suggests the psychological truth that when we are in dire need, it is our dreams of happier times which alone can sustain us.

It is not the words of the text but the colors of the pictures which permit the little mice—and, by proxy, the child who looks at them—to relive in imagination the rays of the sun which warm them, and the colors of the flowers, leaves, and berries which gladden their hearts. The depressing gray that entirely dominates the pictures, indicating the little mice's desperation in hard times, is largely replaced by warm, rich, brighter colors as Frederick recalls for his fellow mice what the world looked like when they were happy. The change of the colors in the pictures persuades the child much more effectively than words could that when our physical existence seems threatened, only spiritual renewal, based on remembrance of happy experiences in the past, can lift our spirits out of depression. Also, it becomes clear that the dreams of the poet and the artist can do more for us when we are seeking renewal than practically anything else.

"Frederick" is not Lionni's only story about the glory of the human spirit. "Swimmy" makes the case for the importance of imaginative coping when we are threatened by overpowering evil forces. This fable tells, again mainly in pictures, how the well-coordinated action of many weak little fishes can drive away the powerful enemy. Swimmy gains this ability to plan for a successful defense through opening himself to the beauty and wonders of the world.

"The Alphabet Tree" shows rather than tells what literacy is all about. It is not rote learning of the letters of the alphabet, or even of words. The letters that grow on the alphabet tree can easily be blown away, as the pictures show; even when we have learned the letters well, they have no staying power in our mind. Further, being able to assemble the letters into simple words does not ensure literacy either. Only when the words begin to say something of real significance to us has the alphabet tree served its purpose: that of providing us with the material of meaning to our existence.

But there is no point in going on to tell in words what these rich and varied stories mean, since their meaning is conveyed so much better by the artist. It is Leo Lionni's wonderful, colorful pictures that stimulate the child's imagination, charming him while educating his mind in the most enjoyable manner. It is the beauty of these pictures that permits the adult reading with his child to participate in what spontaneously captivates the imagination of the child, enriches it, and with it satisfies him emotionally. So it is high time for me to stop writing and let Leo Lionni's consummate artistry speak for itself.

BRUNO BETTELHEIM
March 1985

Frederick

All along the meadow where the cows grazed and the horses ran, there was an old stone wall. In that wall, not far from the barn and the granary, a chatty family of field mice had their home.

But the farmers had moved away, the barn was abandoned, and the granary stood empty. And since winter was not far off, the little mice began to gather corn and nuts and wheat and straw. They all worked day and night.

All—except Frederick.

"Frederick, why don't you work?" they asked.

"I do work," said Frederick. "I gather sunrays for the cold dark winter days."

And when they saw Frederick sitting there, staring at the meadow, they said, "And now, Frederick?"

"I gather colors," answered Frederick simply. "For winter is gray."

And once Frederick seemed half asleep. "Are you dreaming, Frederick?" they asked reproachfully.

But Frederick said, "Oh no, I am gathering words. For the winter days are long and many, and we'll run out of things to say."

The winter days came, and when the first snow fell, the five little field mice took to their hideout in the stones. In the beginning there was lots to eat, and the mice told stories of foolish foxes and silly cats. They were a happy family.

But little by little they had nibbled up most of the nuts and berries, the straw was gone, and the corn was only a memory. It was cold in the wall and no one felt like chatting.

Then they remembered what Frederick had said about sunrays and colors and words. "What about *your* supplies, Frederick?" they asked.

"Close your eyes," said Frederick as he climbed onto a big stone. "Now I send you the rays of the sun. Do you feel how their golden glow . . ."

And as Frederick spoke of the sun the four little mice began to feel warmer. Was it Frederick's voice? Was it magic?

"And how about the colors, Frederick?" they asked anxiously.

"Close your eyes again," Frederick said. And when he told them of the blue periwinkles, the red poppies in the yellow wheat, and the green leaves of the berry bush, they saw the colors as clearly as if they had been painted in their minds.

"And the words, Frederick?"
Frederick cleared his throat, waited
a moment, and then, as if from
a stage, he said:

8

"Who scatters snowflakes? Who melts the ice?
Who spoils the weather? Who makes it nice?
Who grows the four-leaf clovers in June?
Who dims the daylight? Who lights the moon?

Four little field mice who live in the sky.
Four little field mice . . . like you and I.
One is the Springmouse who turns on the showers.
Then comes the Summer who paints in the flowers.
The Fallmouse is next with walnuts and wheat.
And Winter is last . . . with little cold feet.

Aren't we lucky the seasons are four?
Think of a year with one less . . . or one more!"

When Frederick had finished, they all applauded. "But Frederick," they said, "you are a poet!"

Frederick blushed, took a bow, and said shyly, "I know it."

Fish Is Fish

At the edge of the woods there was a pond, and there a minnow and a tadpole swam among the weeds. They were inseparable friends.

One morning the tadpole discovered that during the night he had grown two little legs.

"Look," he said, triumphantly. "Look, I am a frog!"

"Nonsense," said the minnow. "How could you be a frog if only last night you were a little fish, just like me!"

They argued and argued until finally the tadpole said, "Frogs are frogs and fish is fish and that's that!"

In the weeks that followed, the tadpole grew tiny front legs and his tail got smaller and smaller. And then one fine day, a real frog now, he climbed out of the water and onto the grassy bank.

The minnow too had grown and had become a full-fledged fish. He often wondered where his four-footed friend had gone. But days and weeks went by and the frog did not return.

Then one day, with a happy splash that shook the weeds, the frog jumped into the pond.

"Where have you been?" asked the fish excitedly.

"I have been about the world—hopping here and there," said the frog, "and I have seen extraordinary things."

"Like what?" asked the fish.

"Birds," said the frog mysteriously. "Birds!" And he told the fish about the birds, who had wings, and two legs, and many, many colors.

As the frog talked, his friend saw the birds fly through his mind like large feathered fish.

"What else?" asked the fish impatiently.

"Cows," said the frog. "Cows! They have four legs, horns, eat grass, and carry pink bags of milk.

"And people!" said the frog. "Men, women, children!" And he talked
and talked until it was dark in the pond.

But the picture in the fish's mind was full of lights and colors and
marvelous things, and he couldn't sleep. Ah, if he could only jump about
like his friend and see that wonderful world.

And so the days went by. The frog had gone and the fish just
lay there dreaming about birds in flight, grazing cows, and those
strange animals, all dressed up, that his friend called people.

One day he finally decided that come what may, he
too must see them. And so with a mighty whack of
the tail he jumped clear out of the water and onto
the bank. He landed in the dry, warm grass and
there he lay gasping for air, unable to breathe
or to move. "Help," he groaned feebly.

Luckily the frog, who had been hunting butterflies nearby, saw him and with all his strength pushed him back into the pond.

Still stunned, the fish floated about for an instant. Then he breathed deeply, letting the clean, cool water run through his gills. Now he felt weightless again, and with an ever-so-slight motion of the tail he could move to and fro, up and down, as before.

The sunrays reached down within the weeds and gently shifted patches of luminous color. This world was surely the most beautiful of all worlds. He smiled at his friend the frog, who sat watching him from a lily leaf. "You were right," he said. "Fish is fish."

Alexander
and the
Wind-Up Mouse

"Help! Help! A mouse!" There was a scream. Then a crash. Cups, saucers, and spoons were flying in all directions.

Alexander ran for his hole as fast as his little legs would carry him. All he wanted was a few crumbs, and yet every time they saw him they would scream for help or chase him with a broom. ·

One day, when there was no one in the house, Alexander heard a squeak in Annie's room. He sneaked in and what did he see? Another mouse. But not an ordinary mouse like himself. Instead of legs it had two little wheels, and on its back there was a key.

"Who are you?" asked Alexander.

"I am Willy the wind-up mouse, Annie's favorite toy. They wind me to make me run around in circles, they cuddle me, and at night I sleep on a soft white pillow between the doll and a woolly teddy bear. Everyone loves me."

"They don't care much for me," said Alexander sadly. But he was happy to have found a friend. "Let's go to the kitchen and look for crumbs," he said.

"Oh, I can't," said Willy. "I can only move when they wind me. But I don't mind. Everybody loves me."

Alexander, too, came to love Willy. He went to visit him whenever he could. He told him of his adventures with brooms, flying saucers, and mousetraps. Willy talked about the penguin, the woolly bear, and mostly about Annie. The two friends spent many happy hours together.

But when he was alone in the dark of his hideout, Alexander thought of Willy with envy.

"Ah!" he sighed. "Why can't I be a wind-up mouse like Willy and be cuddled and loved."

One day Willy told a strange story. "I've heard," he whispered mysteriously, "that in the garden, at the end of the pebblepath, close to the blackberry bush, there lives a magic lizard who can change one animal to another."

"Do you mean," said Alexander, "that he could change me into a wind-up mouse like you?"

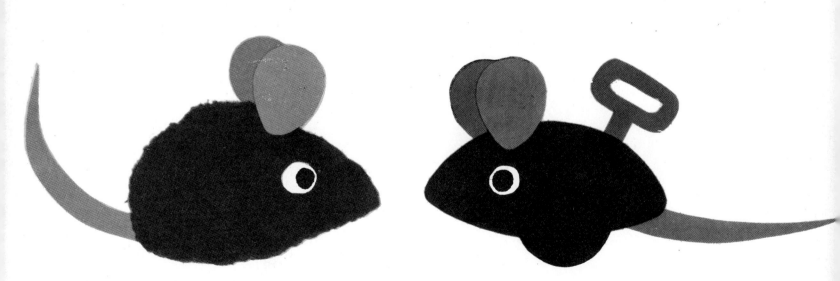

That very afternoon Alexander went into the garden and ran to the end of the path. "Lizard, lizard," he whispered. And suddenly there stood before him, full of the colors of flowers and butterflies, a large lizard. "Is it true that you could change me into a wind-up mouse?" asked Alexander in a quivering voice.

"When the moon is round," said the lizard, "bring me a purple pebble."

For days and days Alexander searched the garden for a purple pebble. In vain. He found yellow pebbles and blue pebbles and green pebbles—but not one tiny purple pebble.

At last, tired and hungry, he returned to the house. In a corner of the pantry he saw a box full of old toys, and there, between blocks and broken dolls, was Willy. "What happened?" said Alexander, surprised.

Willy told him a sad story. It had been Annie's birthday. There had been a party and everyone had brought a gift. "The next day," Willy sighed, "many of the old toys were dumped in this box. We will all be thrown away."

Alexander was almost in tears. "Poor, poor Willy!" he thought. But then suddenly something caught his eye. Could it really be . . . ? Yes, it was! It was a little purple pebble.

All excited, he ran to the garden, the precious pebble tight in his arms. There was a full moon. Out of breath, Alexander stopped near the blackberry bush. "Lizard, lizard, in the bush," he called quickly.

The leaves rustled and there stood the lizard. "The moon is round, the pebble found," said the lizard. "Who or what do you wish to be?"

"I want to be . . . " Alexander stopped. Then suddenly he said, "Lizard, lizard, could you change Willy into a mouse like me?"

The lizard blinked. There was a blinding light. And then all was quiet. The purple pebble was gone.

Alexander ran back to the house as fast as he could. The box was there, but alas it was empty. "Too late," he thought, and with a heavy heart he went to his hole in the baseboard.

Something squeaked! Cautiously Alexander moved closer to the hole. There was a mouse inside. "Who are you?" said Alexander, a little frightened.

"My name is Willy," said the mouse.

"Willy!" cried Alexander. "The lizard . . . the lizard did it!" He hugged Willy and then they ran to the garden path. And there they danced until dawn.

The Biggest House
in the World

Some snails lived on a juicy cabbage. They moved gently around,
carrying their houses from leaf to leaf, in search of a tender spot
to nibble on.

One day a little snail said to his father, "When I grow up I
want to have the biggest house in the world."

"That is silly," said his father, who happened to be
the wisest snail on the cabbage.

"Some things are better small."

And he told this story.

33

Once upon a time, a little snail, just like you, said to his father, "When I grow up I want to have the biggest house in the world."

"Some things are better small," said his father. "Keep your house light and easy to carry."

But the little snail would not listen, and hidden in the shade of a large cabbage leaf, he twisted and twitched, this way and that, until he discovered how to make his house grow.

It grew and grew, and the snails on the cabbage said, "You surely have the biggest house in the world."

The little snail kept on twisting and twitching until his house was as big as a melon. Then, by moving his tail swiftly from left to right, he learned to grow large pointed bulges. And by squeezing and pushing, and by wishing very hard, he was able to add bright colors and beautiful designs.

Now he knew that his was the biggest and the most beautiful house in the whole world. He was proud and happy.

A swarm of butterflies flew overhead.

"Look!" one of them said. "A cathedral!"

"No," said another, "it's a circus!"

They never guessed that what they were looking at was the house of a snail.

And a family of frogs, on their way to a distant pond, stopped in awe. "Never," they later told some cousins, "never have you seen such an amazing sight. An ordinary little snail with a house like a birthday cake."

One day, after they had eaten all the leaves and only a few knobby stems were left, the snails moved to another cabbage. But the little snail, alas, couldn't move. His house was much too heavy.

He was left behind, and with nothing to eat he slowly faded away. Nothing remained but the house. And that too, little by little, crumbled, until nothing remained at all.

That was the end of the story. The little snail was almost in tears.

But then he remembered his own house. "I shall keep it small," he thought, "and when I grow up I shall go wherever I please."

And so one day, light and joyous, he went on to see the world.

Some leaves fluttered lightly in the breeze, and others hung heavily to the ground. Where the dark earth had split, crystals glittered in the early sun. There were polka-dotted mushrooms, and towery stems from which little flowers seemed to wave. There was a pine cone lying in the lacy shade of ferns, and pebbles in a nest of sand, smooth and round like the eggs of the turtledove. Lichen clung to the rocks and bark to the trees. The tender buds were sweet and cool with morning dew.

The little snail was very happy.

The seasons came and went, but the snail never forgot the story his father had told him. And when someone asked, "How come you have such a small house?" he would tell the story of *the biggest house in the world*.

Geraldine, the Music Mouse

Geraldine had never heard music before. Noises, yes. Many noises—the voices of people, the slamming of doors, the barking of dogs, the rushing of water, the meows of cats in the courtyard. And, of course, the soft peeping of mice. But music, never.

Then one morning . . .

In the pantry of the empty house where Geraldine lived, she discovered an enormous piece of Parmesan cheese—the largest she had ever seen. Eagerly, she took a little bite from it. It was delicious. But how would she be able to take it to her secret hideout in the barn?

She ran to her friends who lived next door and told them about her discovery. "If you help me carry it to my hideout," she said, "I'll give each of you a big piece."

Her friends, who loved cheese, happily agreed. "Let's go!" they said. And off they went.

"It's enormous! It's gigantic! It's immense! It's fantastic!" they shouted with joy when they saw the piece of cheese. They pushed and pulled and tugged and finally they managed to carry it to Geraldine's hideout.

There, Geraldine climbed to the very top of the cheese. She dug her little teeth into it and pulled away crumb after crumb, chunk after chunk.

As her friends carried away their cheese tidbits, Geraldine peered in amazement at the hole she had gnawed. There she saw the shapes of two enormous ears—cheese ears!

As soon as her friends were gone, she went back to work again, nibbling away at the cheese as fast as she could. When she was halfway through, Geraldine climbed down to have a look at the forms she had freed. She could hardly believe what she saw. The ears were those of a giant mouse, still partly hidden, of solid cheese. To its puckered lips it held a flute. Geraldine gnawed and gnawed until she had finally uncovered the entire mouse.

Then she realized that the flute was really the tip of the mouse's tail. Astonished, exhausted, and a little frightened, Geraldine stared at the cheese statue. With the dimming of the last daylight she fell asleep.

Suddenly she was awakened by some strange sounds. They seemed to come from the direction of the mouse's flute. She jumped to her feet. As it grew darker, the sounds became clearer and more melodious until they seemed to move lightly through the air like invisible strings of silver and gold. Never had Geraldine heard anything so beautiful.

"Music!" she thought. "This must be music!"

She listened all through the night until the first glow of dawn filtered through the dusty windowpanes. But as the cheese mouse was slowly bathed in light, the music became softer, until it stopped altogether.

"Play, play," Geraldine begged. "Play some more!"

But not a sound came from the flute.

"Will it ever play again?" Geraldine thought as she gobbled up some of the crumbs that lay around.

When the next evening approached, it brought the answer to her question. The music began faintly at dusk and lasted until the break of day. And so, night after night, the cheese flutist played for Geraldine. She learned to recognize the melodies, and even in daylight they lingered in her ears.

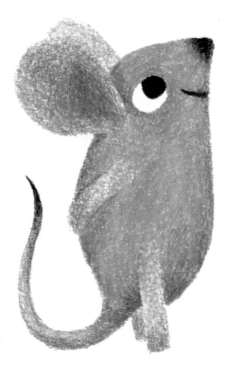

Then one day she met her friends on the street. They were desperate.

"Geraldine!" they said. "We have no more food, and there is none to be found anywhere. You must share your cheese with us."

"But that is not possible!" Geraldine shouted.

"Why?" asked the others angrily.

"Because . . . because . . . because it is MUSIC!"

Her friends looked at Geraldine, surprised. "What is music?" they asked all together.

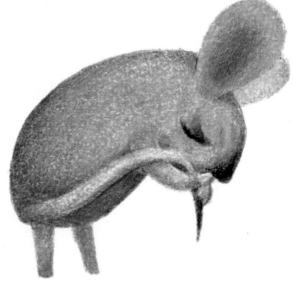

For a moment Geraldine stood deep
in thought. Then she took a step backward,
solemnly lifted the tip of her tail to her puckered lips,
took a deep breath, and blew. She blew hard. She
puffed, she peeped, she tweeted, she screeched.
Her friends laughed until their hungry little
tummies hurt.

Then a long, soft, beautiful whistle came from Geraldine's lips. One of the melodies of the cheese flute echoed in the air. The little mice held their breath in amazement. Other mice came to hear the miracle. When the tune came to an end, Gregory, the oldest of the group, whispered, "If this is music, Geraldine, you are right. We cannot eat that cheese."

"No," said Geraldine joyfully. "Now we CAN eat the cheese. Because . . . now the music is in me."

With that they all followed Geraldine to the barn. And while Geraldine whistled the gayest of tunes, they ate cheese to their tummies' content.

Tico
and the
Golden Wings

*Many years ago I knew a little bird whose name was Tico. He would
sit on my shoulder and tell me all about the flowers, the ferns, and
the tall trees. Once Tico told me this story about himself.*

I don't know how it happened, but when I was young I had no wings.
I sang like the other birds and I hopped like them, but I couldn't fly.

Luckily my friends loved me. They flew from tree to tree, and in the
evening they brought me berries and tender fruits gathered from the
highest branches.

Often I asked myself, "Why can't I fly like the other birds? Why
can't I, too, soar through the big blue sky over villages and treetops?"

And I dreamed that I had golden wings, strong enough to carry me
over the snow-capped mountains far away.

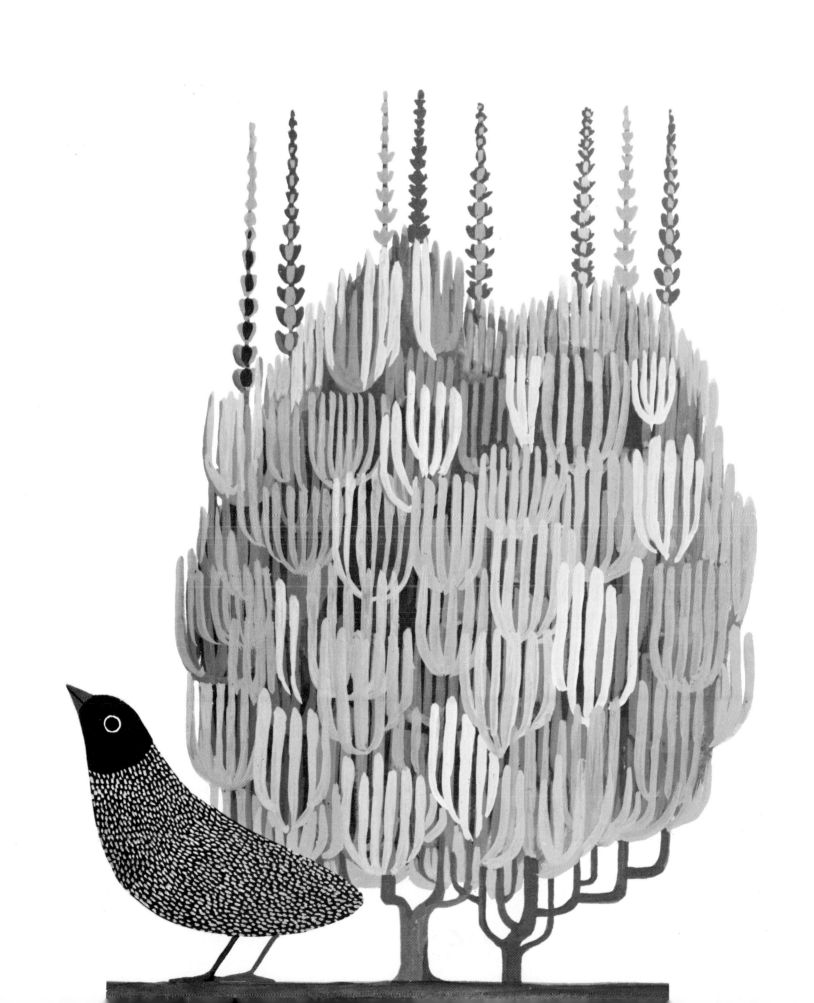

One summer night I was awakened by a noise nearby. A strange bird, pale as a pearl, was standing behind me.

"I am the wishingbird," he said. "Make a wish and it will come true."

I remembered my dreams and with all my might I wished I had a pair of golden wings. Suddenly there was a flash of light and on my back there were wings, golden wings, shimmering in the moonlight. The wishingbird had vanished.

Cautiously I flapped my wings. And then I flew. I flew higher than the tallest tree. The flower patches below looked like stamps scattered over the countryside, and the river like a silver necklace lying in the meadows. I was happy and I flew well into the day.

But when my friends saw me swoop down from the sky, they frowned on me and said, "You think you are better than we are, don't you, with those golden wings. You wanted to be *different*." And off they flew without saying another word.

Why had they gone? Why were they angry? Was it *bad* to be different? I could fly as high as the eagle. Mine were the most beautiful wings in the world. But my friends had left me and I was very lonely.

One day I saw a man sitting in front of a hut. He was a basket maker and there were baskets all around him.

There were tears in his eyes. I flew onto a branch from where I could speak to him.

"Why are you sad?" I asked.

"Oh, little bird, my child is sick and I am poor. I cannot buy the medicines that would make him well."

"How can I help him?" I thought. And suddenly I knew. "I will give him one of my feathers."

"How can I thank you!" said the poor man happily. "You have saved my child. But look! Your wing!"

Where the golden feather had been, there was a real black feather, as soft as silk.

From that day, little by little, I gave my golden feathers away and black feathers appeared in their place.

I bought many presents: three new puppets for a poor puppeteer, a spinning wheel to spin the yarn for an old woman's shawl, a compass for a fisherman who got lost at sea . . .

And when I had given my last golden feathers to a beautiful bride,
my wings were as black as India ink.

I flew to the big tree where my friends gathered for the night.
Would they welcome me?

They chirped with joy. "Now you are just like us," they said.

We all huddled close together. But I was so happy and excited, I couldn't sleep. I remembered the basket maker's son, the old woman, the puppeteer, and all the others I had helped with my feathers.

"Now my wings are black," I thought, "and yet I am not like my friends. We are *all* different. Each for his own memories, and his own invisible golden dreams."

Cornelius

When the eggs hatched, the little crocodiles crawled out onto the riverbeach. But Cornelius walked out *upright*.

As he grew taller and stronger he rarely came down on all fours. He saw things no other crocodile had ever seen before. "I can see far beyond the bushes!" he said.

But the others said, "What's so good about that?"

"I can see the fish from above!" Cornelius said.

"So what?" said the others, annoyed.

And so one day Cornelius angrily decided to walk away.

It was not long before he met a monkey. "I can walk upright!" Cornelius said proudly. "And I can see things far away!"

"I can stand on my head," said the monkey. "And hang from my tail."

Cornelius was amazed. "Could I learn to do that?" he asked.

"Of course," replied the monkey. "All you need is a lot of hard work and a little help."

Cornelius worked hard at learning the monkey's tricks, and the monkey seemed happy to help him. When he had finally learned to stand on his head and hang from his tail, Cornelius walked proudly back to the riverbeach.

"Look!" he said. "I can stand on my head."
"So what!" was all the others said.
"And I can hang from my tail!" said Cornelius.
But the others just frowned and repeated,
    "So what!"

69

Disappointed and angry, Cornelius decided to go back to the monkey. But just as he had turned around, he looked back. And what did he see?

There the others were, falling all over themselves trying to stand on their heads and hang from their tails! Cornelius smiled. Life on the riverbeach would never be the same again.

Swimmy

A happy school of little fish lived in a corner of the sea somewhere.
They were all red. Only one of them was as black as a mussel shell.
He swam faster than his brothers and sisters.
His name was Swimmy.

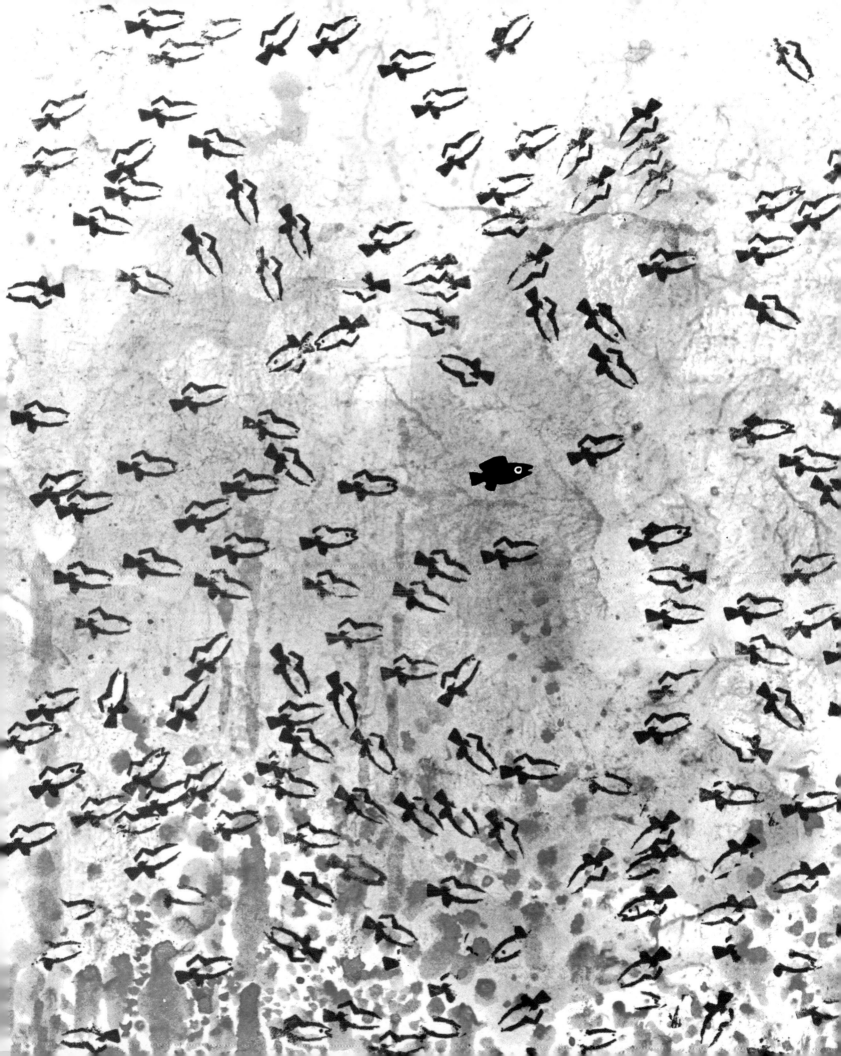

One bad day a tuna fish, swift, fierce, and very hungry, came darting through the waves. In one gulp he swallowed all the little red fish.

Only Swimmy escaped. He swam away in the deep wet world. He was scared, lonely, and very sad.

But the sea was full of wonderful creatures, and as he swam from marvel to marvel Swimmy was happy again.

He saw a medusa made of rainbow jelly; a lobster, who walked about like a water-moving machine; strange fish, pulled by an invisible thread;

a forest of seaweeds growing from sugar-candy rocks; an eel whose tail was almost too far away to remember; and sea anemones, who looked like pink palm trees swaying in the wind.

Then, hidden in the dark shade of rocks and weeds, he saw a school of little fish, just like his own.

"Let's go and swim and play and SEE things!" he said happily.

"We can't," said the little red fish. "The big fish will eat us all."

"But you can't just lie there," said Swimmy. "We must THINK of something."

Swimmy thought and thought and thought. Then suddenly he said, "I have it! We are going to swim all together like the biggest fish in the sea!"

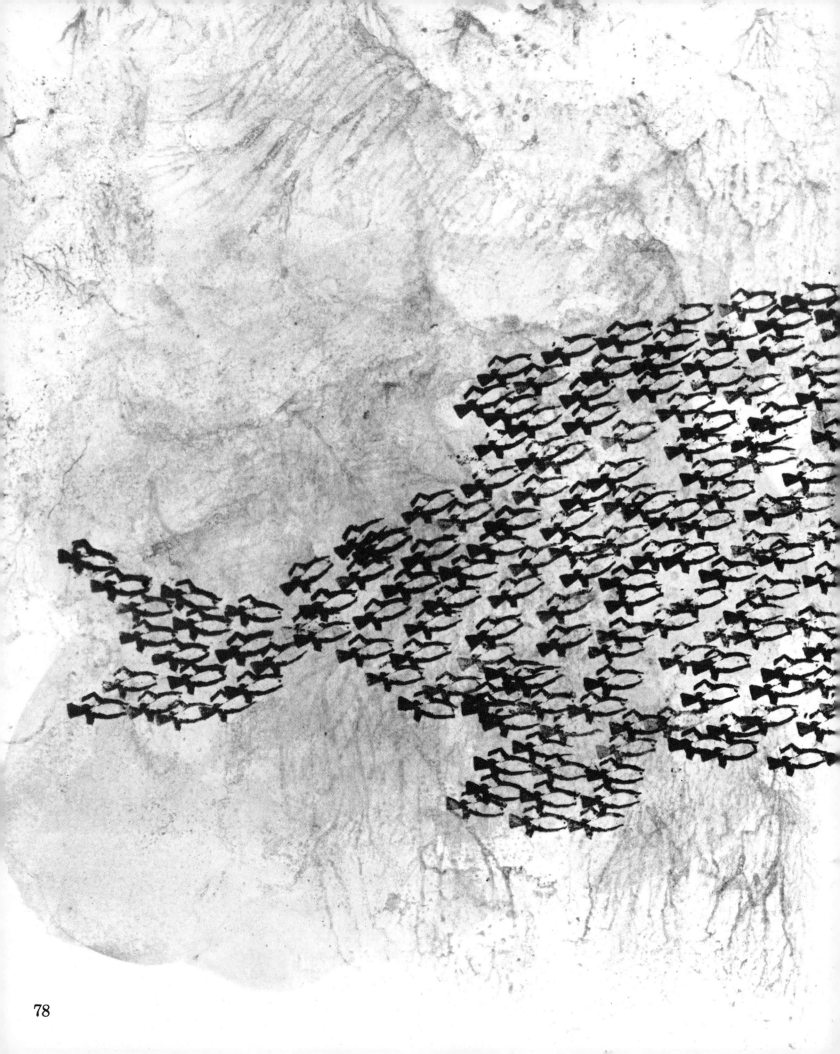

He taught them to swim close together, each in his own place,
and when they had learned to swim like one giant fish, he said,
"I'll be the eye."

And so they swam in the cool morning water and in the midday sun and chased the big fish away.

In the Rabbitgarden

The rabbitgarden was surely the most beautiful garden, and the two little rabbits the happiest bunnies, in the world.

One day the old rabbit called them. "I am going away for a while," he said in a raucous voice. "Behave well, and remember—eat all the carrots you want, but don't touch the apples or the fox will get you."

The two little rabbits ran back to play, and when they were hungry they dug up a carrot or two. The next day they dug here and they dug there, but they couldn't find a single carrot. "What will we do now?" they said, and tears came to their eyes.

Suddenly they saw a beautiful big carrot, half hidden by the trunk of an apple tree. They grabbed it eagerly, but—*whoops!*—it disappeared.

And there in front of them was an enormous serpent.

"Were you going to eat the tip of my tail?" he said. "Do little rabbits eat serpents nowadays?" And he laughed, "Ha! Ha! Ha!"

"Sorry," mumbled the bunnies, confused and a little scared. "We thought the tip of your tail was a carrot. We are hungry and there isn't a carrot to be found anywhere."

"Carrots, carrots," laughed the serpent. "With all the beautiful apples that hang in the apple tree!"

"We can't reach them," said the bunnies. "And besides—"

But before they could say "the old rabbit" the serpent presented them with the reddest, most fragrant apple they had ever seen or smelled. And was it good! When they had eaten their fill, the serpent said, "And now let's play!"

In the days that followed, the three became the best of friends. The serpent invented tricks and games. They rolled down slopes together, and he bounced them up into the air. And when they were hungry he picked them the ripest apples.

One morning the two little rabbits awoke with a jolt. There, peering out at them, half hidden in the weeds, was a big red fox. For a moment they felt as if they were frozen to the ground. Then they leaped for their lives. The fox followed close on their heels and was just about to catch them when . . .

there was the serpent waiting for them, his mouth wide open. The little rabbits understood at once. With a thump they plunged right into the serpent.

The fox had never seen such a fearful animal. "A dragon!" he cried. He turned around and ran right back where he had come from.

Then one fine day the old rabbit returned from his trip. He couldn't believe his eyes. Two happy little bunnies who ate apples! A smiling serpent! He was so surprised that he forgot to be angry.

The bunnies told him all about the serpent and how he had scared away the fox.

"Hmmm . . ." said the old rabbit, thinking about what he had heard.

Then the serpent picked the juiciest apple he could find.

"Okay," said the old rabbit, smiling. "Maybe apples are just big, round, shiny carrots that hang from carrot trees," and in a jiffy he gobbled up the apple, skin and all.

Theodore
and the
Talking Mushroom

In the stump of an old oak there lived four friends—a lizard, a frog, a turtle, and a mouse called Theodore.

"Any time I lose my tail I can grow a new one," boasted the lizard.

"I can swim under water," said the frog.

"I can close like a box," said the turtle.

"And you?" they asked the mouse.

Theodore, who was always afraid, blushed. "I can run," he said. The others laughed, "Ha! Ha! Ha!"

One day Theodore was frightened by a leaf that came fluttering down from a tree. "An owl!" he thought as he ran for cover.

Luckily he found a huge mushroom to hide under. He was too frightened to notice that it was as blue as an August sky. Theodore hid for a long time. He was tired. He had almost fallen asleep, when suddenly he was startled by a strange noise. "Quirp!"

Theodore looked around, his little heart beating wildly. But all was quiet. "I must have dreamed it," he thought as he returned to the cool shade of the mushroom. He dozed off softly, when suddenly there was that noise again—"Quirp!"

It was the mushroom! Theodore was too excited to be frightened. "Can you talk?" he gasped. The mushroom did not answer, but after a little while it made the noise again. And again. Soon Theodore realized that the mushroom could not really speak. It could only say "Quirp."

Then he had an idea.

He went back to his friends. "I have something important to tell you," he said mysteriously. "Some time ago I discovered a talking mushroom. The only one in the whole world. It is the Mushroom of Truth and I have learned to understand its language."

He guided his friends toward the edge of the woods. There stood the blue mushroom.

"Mushroom, speak!" Theodore commanded.

"Quirp!" said the mushroom.

"What does it mean?" asked Theodore's friends, dumbfounded.

"It means," said Theodore, "that the mouse should be venerated above all other animals."

"Quirp!"

The news of Theodore's discovery spread quickly. His friends made him a crown. Animals came from far away with garlands of flowers.

Theodore was no longer afraid. He did not have to run—he did not even have to walk. Wherever he went he was carried on the turtle's back on a cushion of flowers. And wherever he went he was venerated above all other animals.

One day he and his three friends went on a trip. They went far beyond the edge of the woods through the fields of heather. There lay the hills they had never crossed. The frog jumped ahead. Suddenly, from the top of the hill,

he shouted,

"Look! Look!"

The valley below was filled with hundreds of blue mushrooms!
And a chorus of "Quirps" filled the air.

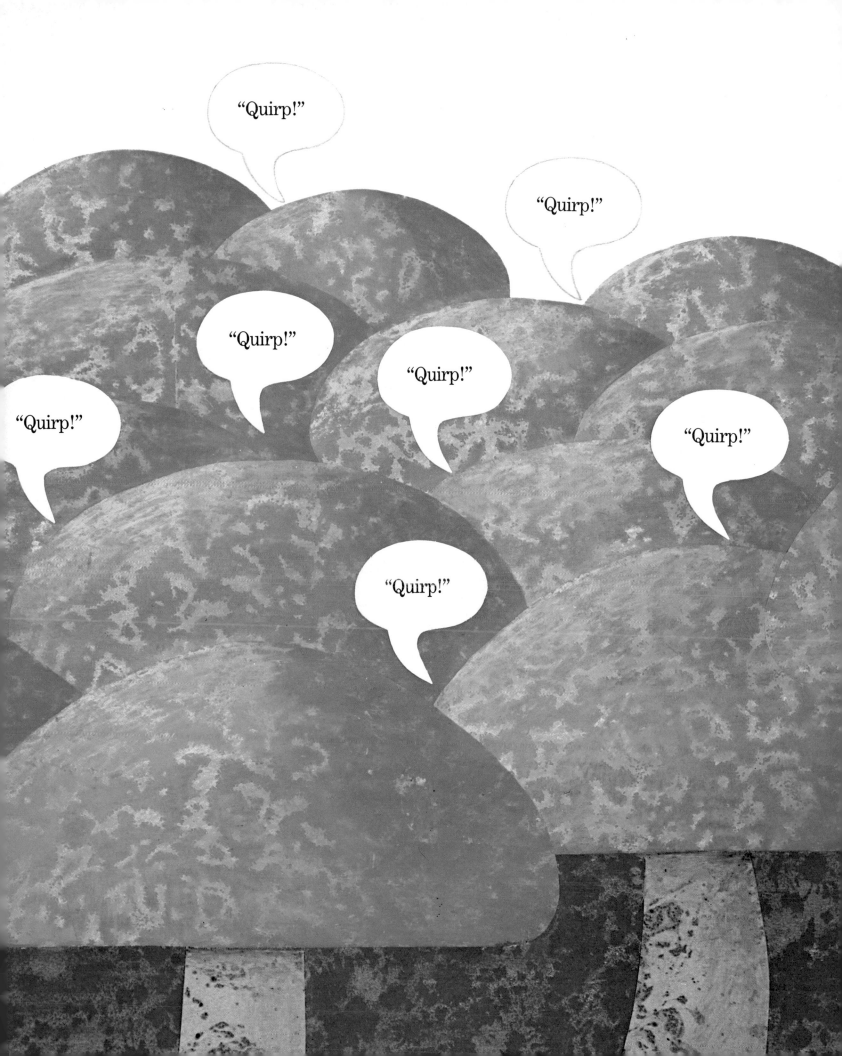

Speechless and bewildered, they all gaped at the unexpected sight. Theodore knew he should say something, but the words failed him and he just stood there trembling and stammering. Then his friends exploded with anger.

"Liar!" "Faker!" "Fraud!" they shouted.

"Charlatan!" "Scoundrel!" "Imposter!"

Theodore ran as he had never run before. Through the woods,
past the blue mushroom, past the old oak stump . . .

He ran and ran. And his friends never saw him again.

A Color of His Own

Elephants are gray.
Goldfish are red.
Parrots are green.
Pigs are pink.

All animals have a color of their own, except chameleons. They change color wherever they go.

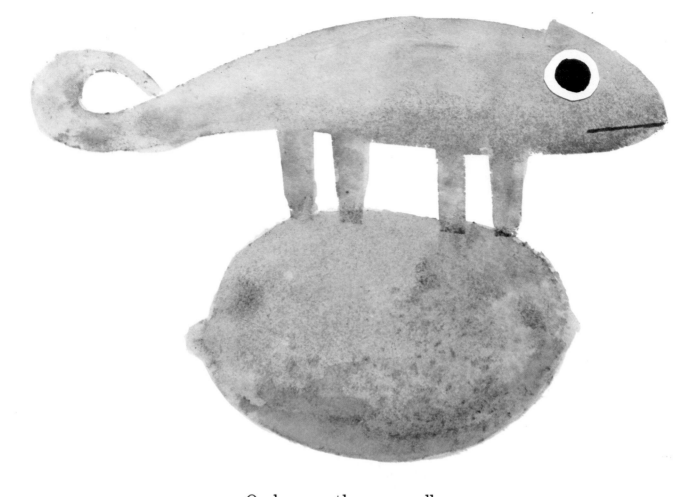

On lemons they are yellow.
In the heather they are purple.
And on the tiger they are striped like tigers.

108

One day a chameleon who was sitting on a tiger's tail said to himself, "If I remain on a leaf I shall be green forever, and so I too, will have a color of my own." With this thought he cheerfully climbed onto the greenest leaf.

But in autumn the leaf turned yellow—and so did the chameleon. Later the leaf turned red, and the chameleon, too, turned red. And then the winter winds blew the leaf from the branch and with it the chameleon.

The chameleon was black in the long winter night. But when spring came, he walked out into the green grass. And there he met another chameleon.

He told his sad story. "Won't we ever have a color of our own?" he asked.

"I'm afraid not," said the other chameleon, who was older and wiser. "But," he added, "why don't we stay together? We will still change color wherever we go, but you and I will always be alike."

And so they remained side by side.

They were green together,
and purple,
and yellow,

and red with white polka dots.

And they lived happily ever after.

The Greentail Mouse

In the quietest corner of the Willshire woods a community of field mice lived a peaceful life. There were sweet berries, juicy roots, and tender shoots to eat. The winter days were mild, and during the long summer a cool breeze played softly in the grass. No fox or snake ever discovered the hideout where the little friends had a fine time, day after day.

One spring morning a city mouse came passing through.

"Tell us all about the city," the field mice asked him.

"Most of the time it's sad and dangerous," he answered. "But there is one wonderful day."

"When?" asked the mice.

"Mardi Gras," said the city mouse with an air of mystery and importance. "That's French for Fat Tuesday. On Mardi Gras there is lots of music, and people dance in the streets." And he told them about parades, confetti, streamers, horns that make funny noises—and masks!

"Let's have a Fat Tuesday too!" exclaimed the mice excitedly.

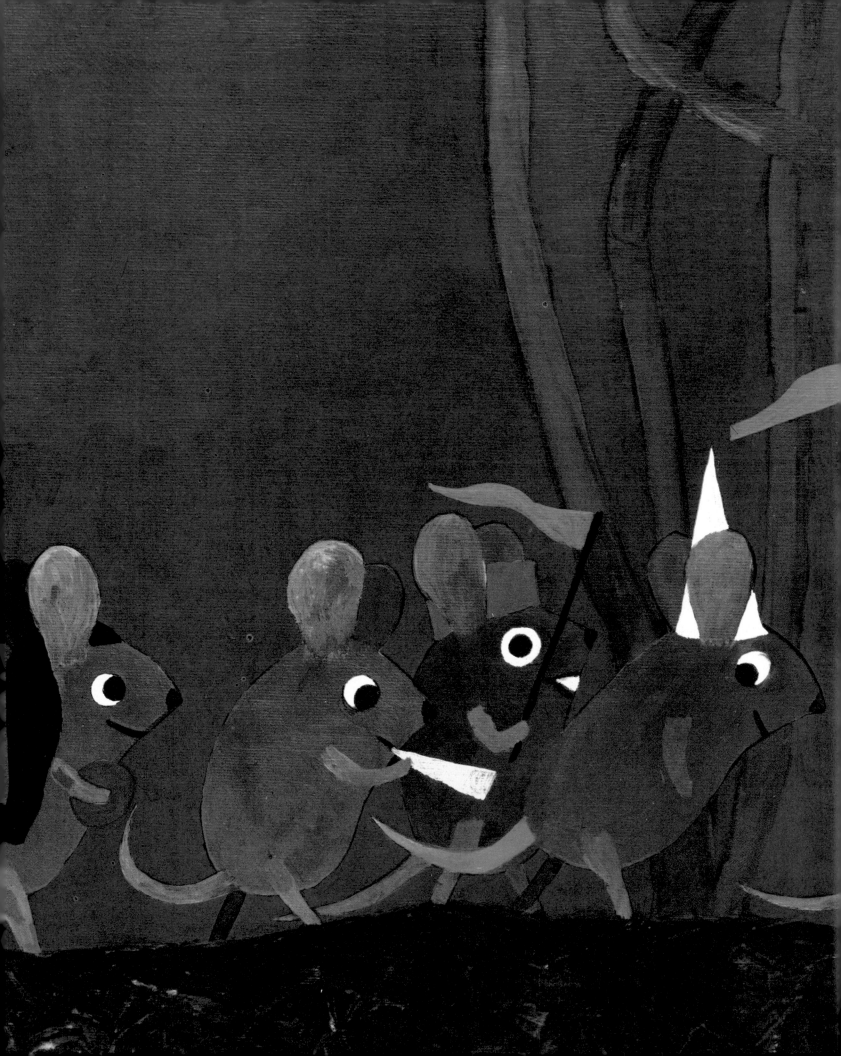

That very afternoon they met at the big pebble. They all agreed that it would be nice to have a Mardi Gras. "We'll decorate the bushes, we'll have a parade and a ball, and at midnight we'll put on masks."

They worked and worked. They cut leaves into ribbons, which they hung from the low branches of trees and bushes. They gathered straw and lichens and petals and made masks of ferocious animals with glittering teeth and fierce eyes.

In the early evening they went to the place they had chosen for the big event. Most of them wore a wig or a hat, and one mouse had even painted her tail green.

"I am the Greentail Mouse," she said with a squeaky voice.

They danced and sang and had a wonderful time until the moon was at its highest point in the sky.

Then they disappeared into the dark bushes and put on their masks. From behind tree trunks and stones they scared each other with ferocious grunts and shouts and shrieks, and threatened each other with sharp teeth and tusks.

Little by little they forgot that they were sweet, harmless mice. They forgot about Mardi Gras and singing and dancing and being joyful. They *really* believed that they were ferocious animals.

"Waoo! Waoo!" yelled the Greentail Mouse from the branch onto which she had climbed.

Everyone was afraid of everyone else, and as the days went by, the once peaceful community became a place full of hate and suspicion.

One morning they saw a strange and frightening sight—*a mouse as tall as the elephant*. A giant mouse! At first they thought that it was a mouse masked as a mouse, but when they realized that it wore no mask at all, they were very frightened and ran as fast as they could. The mouse ran after them, and since he did not have the weight of a mask to carry, he easily overtook them.

"What are you afraid of?" he said. "Have you forgotten what a real mouse is like?"

"But you are the tallest mouse in the world! A giant mouse," the others said, still out of breath.

The mouse laughed. "Nonsense," he said. "If you take off those silly masks you will all be giant mice."

Timidly they removed their masks, one by one, and they realized that the mouse had been right. It was good to be themselves again— real mice, not afraid of one another and eager to have a happy time.

That night they decided to build a big fire and burn all the masks.

"This is better than Fat Tuesday," they said as the masks turned into ashes, and sparks of many colors rose into the sky.

By the time the fire had died out, no one would ever have suspected what had happened, for everything was the way it had been before.

Except for the Greentail Mouse. She just couldn't get her tail clean. She tried the rain and the water in the stream. She scratched and nibbled. She finally gave up. And when someone asked her why she had a green tail, she would shrug her shoulders and simply say, "I was the Greentail Mouse at Mardi Gras."

"What is Mardi Gras?" the other would ask.

"That's French for Fat Tuesday." And she would tell about parades, streamers, and horns that make funny noises. But she never said a word about the ferocious masks. They were tucked far away in her memory, almost forgotten, like a bad dream.

The Alphabet Tree

"This is the Alphabet Tree," said the ant.

"Why is it called the Alphabet Tree?" asked his friend.

"Because not so long ago this tree was full of letters. They lived a happy life, hopping from leaf to leaf on the highest twigs. Each letter had its favorite leaf, where it would sit in the sun and rock in the gentle breeze of spring.

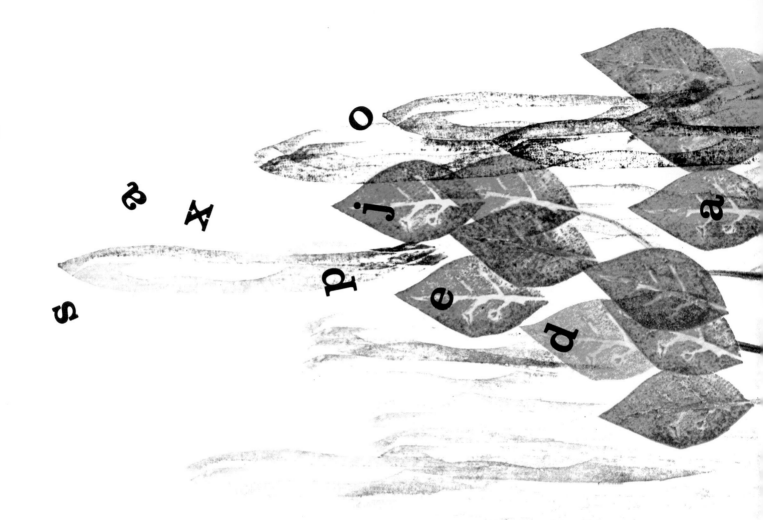

"One day the breeze became a strong gust and the gust became a gale. The letters clung to the leaves with all their might—but some were blown away, and the others were very frightened.

"When the storm had passed, they huddled together in fear, deep in the foliage of the lower branches.

"A funny bug, red and black with
bright yellow wings, saw them
there, hiding in the shade.
" 'We are hiding from the wind,'
the letters explained. 'But
who are you?'

" 'I am the word-bug,' the bug answered. 'I can teach you to make words. If you get together in threes and fours, and even more, no wind will be strong enough to blow you away.'

"Patiently he taught the letters to join together and make words. Some made short and easy words like *dog* and *cat*; others learned to make more difficult ones: *twig*, *leaf*, and even *earth*.

"Happily they climbed back onto the highest leaves, and when the wind came they held on without fear. The word-bug had been right.

"Then, one summer morning, a strange caterpillar appeared amid the foliage. He was purple, woolly, and very large. 'Such confusion!' said the caterpillar when he saw the words scattered around the leaves. 'Why don't you get together and make sentences—and *mean* something?'

"The letters had never thought of this. Now they could really write— *say* things. They said things about the wind, the leaves, the bug.

the wind is bad

the leaves are green

the bug is small

" 'Good!' said the caterpillar approvingly.
'But not good enough.'

" 'Why?' asked the letters, surprised.

" 'Because you must say something *important*,'
said the caterpillar.

"The letters tried to think of something important, *really* important.
Finally they knew what to say. What could be more important than
peace? PEACE ON EARTH AND GOODWILL TOWARD ALL
MEN, they spelled excitedly.

" 'Great!' said the caterpillar. 'Now climb onto my back.'

vill toward all men

"One by one the letters climbed onto the woolly
back. 'But where are you taking us?' they asked
anxiously as the caterpillar began climbing down
the tree.

" 'To the President,' said the caterpillar."